BUZZY

the bumblebee

by Denise Brennan-Nelson
and Illustrated by
Michael Glenn Monroe

SANDY CREEK

This 2009 edition published by Sandy Creek,
by arrangement with Sleeping Bear Press.

Sandy Creek
122 Fifth Avenue
New York, NY 10011

ISBN: 978-1-4351-1695-5

Printed and bound in China.

1 3 5 7 9 10 8 6 4 2

I would like to dedicate this book to my wife
Colleen who has always supported my decision
to be an artist, and to my children, Natalie and
Matthew, who help me remember what it is like
to see the world through the eyes of a child.

Michael Glenn Monroe

To Mom and Dad your love never ends.
To Jackie Wallace my bumblebee friend.
To Rebecca and Rachel with beautiful wings.
To Bob forever, you make my heart sing!
To my buddies, the "foxes," friends always we'll be.
To my seven spirited siblings for encouraging me!
To Heather and all who gave this book wings
Thank you! I wish you beautiful things!

Denise Brennan-Nelson

One sunny day, in a beautiful garden,
there sat a bumblebee named Buzzy.
His stripes were black and yellow,
and his coat was rather fuzzy.

Buzzy liked to fly
like all Bumblebees.
He danced with the flowers
and swayed with the breeze.

He also liked to read
and thought himself worldly and wise,
So Buzzy was startled when he read,
"Bumblebees weren't made to fly."

He read it over and over
"Bumblebees weren't made to fly?"
...According to studies and research
and it went on to explain why.

"Their wing span is wrong
and their bodies are too big."
Buzzy was confused. He thought
"I am not a pig!"

Buzzy couldn't believe what he read
and kept thinking, "Can these facts be true?
I've been flying all this time and
I shouldn't have been able to?"

He tried to make his wings work
by pumping with all of his might.
But the words he had read were stuck in his head,
and now something wasn't right.

Buzzy was stranded on top of a flower,
longing to fly away.
His heart still knew how
but his head had forgotten the way.

Buzzy was scared! "How will I get down
now that I can't fly anymore?"
"I'll have to climb down," he decided,
something he'd never done before.

With book in tow and little heart pounding,
Buzzy tentatively took the first step.
Then very, very, slowly
down the flower he crept.

Buzzy's foot started to slip
and he felt himself letting go...

OH NOOOOO!!!!!

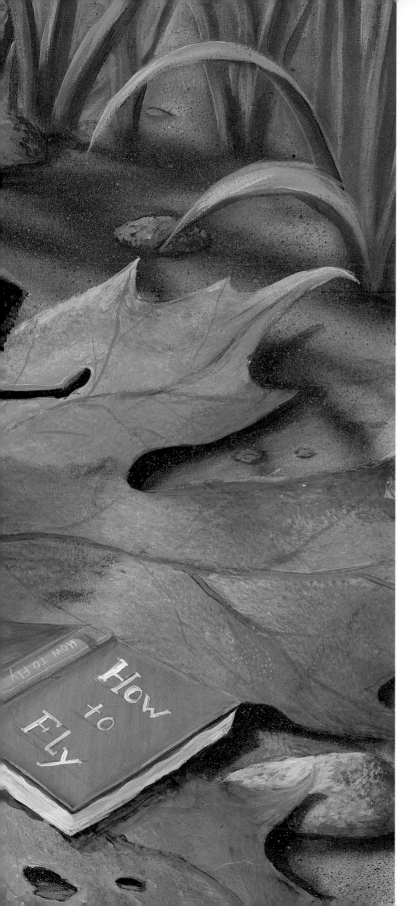

Thank goodness for a leaf,
it helped cushion the blow.

Dazed, Buzzy slowly sat up
thinking, "What should I do now?
My home is so far away,
I've got to get there somehow!"

Two dragonflies saw Buzzy walking
and they asked, "What's wrong with you?"
Buzzy sadly told them
"My flying days are through!"

They didn't understand his problem.
Because their wings worked just fine.
"Would you walk with me?" Buzzy asked,
"No, thank you," they declined.

Feeling very envious
and even a little mad,
Buzzy had a funny feeling inside,
he wanted what they had.

Heavy hearted, he trudged on,
anxious to get home.
Buzzy needed his family
he felt so all-alone!

Just then, Buzzy saw a stream and cried out in frustration, "Now that I can't fly anymore, will I ever reach my destination?"

"Every problem has a solution,"
his mother always said.
Buzzy had to find an answer—
he'd have to use his head.

At that very moment,
a flower petal drifted by.
It gently floated to the river's edge
as Buzzy let out a sigh.

Buzzy had an idea!!!
"I need something that will float."
Looking at the petal in the water
he thought, "That could be my boat."

He picked up a blue jay's feather
and cautiously pushed himself out.
When Buzzy realized the petal would work,
he gave a joyful shout!

As he safely reached the other side
Buzzy was filled with relief...

until he saw the tall, tall grass
and was suddenly overcome with grief.

Sadly, he remembered the days,
when above the grass he would soar.
Once again he thought, "What will I do
now that I can't fly anymore?"

Peering through the thick green grass
Buzzy thought, "This just isn't fair!"
About to give up, he heard a voice say:
"Don't stop! You're almost there."

He looked up to see where it came from,
but his eyes met only the sun.
Mustering all the energy he had left,
Buzzy began to run.

Buzzy burst through the door
with a tear in his eye,
"Mom and Dad, why didn't you tell me
bumblebees weren't made to fly?"

"Why Buzzy," they said,
"You certainly can fly!
Until now, that is,
and do you know why?"

"You're doubting yourself,
fear is blocking the way.
Listen to your heart Buzzy,
not to what others say."

"Ignore labels and limits,
they seldom do good,
they make you think you can't
when inside you know you could!"

Buzzy thought about what they had said
and knew his parents were right.
*It's belief in ourselves
that helps us take flight.*

Quickly, Buzzy ran out the door
and looked up at the sky.
Bursting with confidence and desire
Buzzy shouted, "I want to fly!"

Buzzy's wings fluttered
and his spirit began to soar.
Buzzy knew he would be all right,
he would fly once more.

And sure enough Buzzy flew.
And do you know why?

By believing that he could,
Buzzy was able to fly!